by Chantelle Saumier

illustrated by Vanessa Steunenberg

VINNIE!

STAR OF THE SHOW

ISBN

978-1-4602-3098-5 (Hardcover)

978-1-4602-1741-2 (Paperback)

978-1-4602-1742-9 (eBook)

Produced by:

FriesenPress

Suite 300 – 852 Fort Street

Victoria, BC, Canada V8W 1H8

www.friesenpress.com

Distributed to the trade by The Ingram Book Company

DEDICATED To: My husband, whose unwavering support and love is a driving force behind everything I do. To Evan and Brooklynn, whose imagination and creativity spark my own every day. Last but not least, to Vinnie, our dog.

SPECIAL THANKS To: my family and friends for sharing excitement in my dream. Also to Division 14 at R.C.Garnett for being my first real audience and for your genuine enthusiasm about my stories.

Have you ever heard the expression,

"Dogs are man's best friend"?

If you have a dog, you will probably agree. Dogs really are one of the greatest pets because they give us so much.

They give us love. They give us friendship. They give us happiness, even on our saddest days. And sometimes—just sometimes—they can give us a whole lot of **Trouble**. Or at least my dog can.

Hi! Since you are already here, let me introduce you to him, (my dog that is)—the very dog that came into my life completely by surprise and changed it forever.

Are you ready to meet him?

Are you sure?

Okay then, you asked for it. Without any further delay...

I guess right about now you might be
wondering, "Where did Vinnie come from?"
Great question! So let me tell you.

It all started at
a farmers' market in
a little town close
to where my family
and I spend our
summer vacation
at the cabin.

Now when I say, "my family and I," I mean my whole family—grandparents, aunts, uncles, and cousins all together in one spot for the summer! Throw in two dogs, Parker and Toby, and welcome to **Chaos!**

One day we all decided to go into town to visit the market. So off we went in three separate cars, leaving Parker and Toby to stand guard like the vicious attack dogs they are.

Okay, maybe **not** that vicious!

Since everyone was looking for something different at the market, we decided to split up, leaving my children, their dad, and me free to explore the wonderful sights and scents that surrounded us. At one stand the yummy smell of freshly baked bread and cookies tempted our stomachs.

Mmmm!

At another stand
the flowery fragrance
of handmade soaps
lured us in.

AHHH!

FRESH VEGETABLES

SOAP

Lotion

MADE

AP

At yet another the smell of
crisp vegetables delighted us.

YUM!

It was a nose's dreamland until we suddenly came across
another smell. It was the powerful and unpleasant smell of...

wait for it...

doggie doo!

Pee-yew!

What? **Doggie doo?** Yes, you read that correctly!

There, in the middle of the market, the local pet shelter had set up a stand of their own hoping to convince people to adopt the abandoned dogs in their care. When we saw the dogs, we noticed two cute little six-week-old husky-shepherd puppies peering out of a crate. One in particular looked very lonely and very shy. He had a white stripe running down his nose, was roly-poly, and just like the other dogs there, needed a loving family to take him home.

Little did I know that my family would be the one to do it. After all, we weren't exactly looking for a **PUPPY**

—we were looking for **FRESH VEGETABLES!**

"Please, Mom," begged the kids. "We promise to look after him," they pleaded some more. "We'll even help train him!"

Well, I'm not sure what worked more, the children's puppy-dog eyes or Vinnie's. Whichever it was, we left the farmers' market that day, not with a bushel of carrots, but with **VINNIE** instead. How were we going to explain that to the rest of the family?

Turns out, we weren't the only ones in the family that had some explaining to do! Imagine our surprise when we got back to the cabin and were greeted by a puppy named Lily, and an adult dog named Turtle. Both had been adopted from the market that day too. So in one afternoon, we went from two dogs to five dogs, and the troublesome four-legged gang was born.

UH-OH!

Now, Vinnie is one year old and is not exactly your average-looking dog. He is still very busy growing into his body. That's why most of his body parts seem a little too long and a lot too skinny.

Picture a **HOT DOG** on **STILTS**, and that's Vinnie!

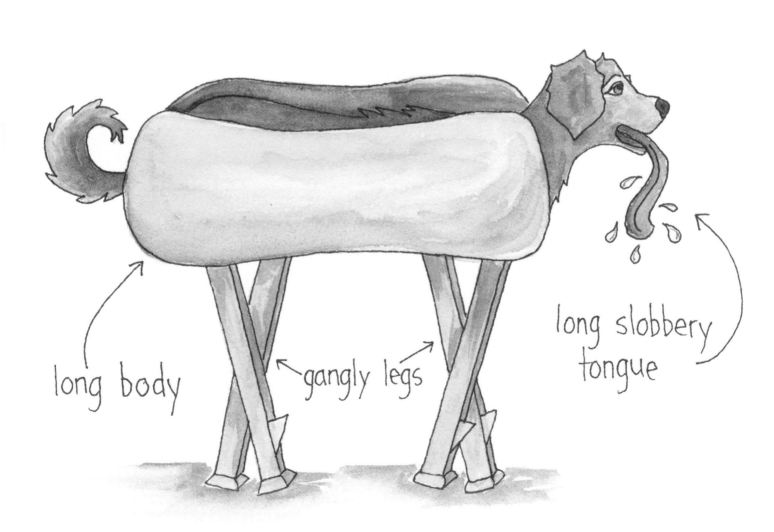

long body

gangly legs

long slobbery tongue

With such a long body, life can sometimes be a little tricky for Vinnie, especially running. Running is tough when you keep tripping over your own legs.

You try running on **stilts!**

Sleeping with long legs is even trickier because they don't tuck in very well,

and they always hang off the bed.

That's okay—Vinnie has solved this problem: he sleeps with all four legs sticking straight in the air.

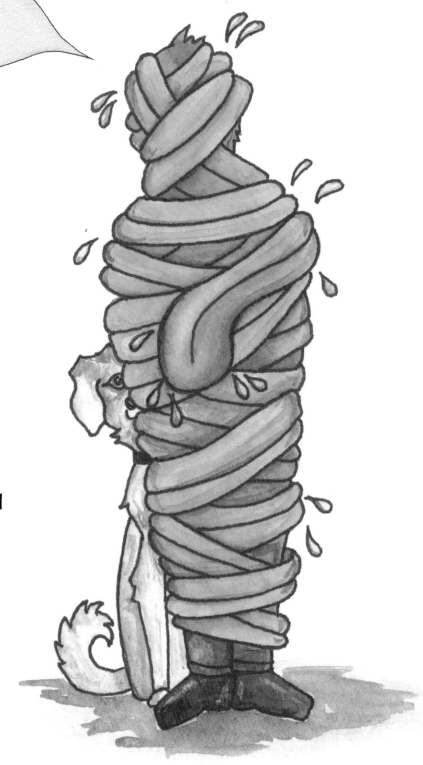

Then there is his
supersized tongue.
You don't want
to get licked by
that thing.

**Trust me, I've been
slimed many times!**

Even though Vinnie
looks a little awkward
right now, we still
think he's the cutest
dog in the world.

When it comes to Vinnie, there are two important things to know about him. Let's call them Vinnie facts.

Vinnie fact #1

Vinnie loves to be loved!

What does he do to get our love?

* nudges our arms,
* puts his head in our laps,
* stares with puppy-dog eyes

How can we resist that?

Beware, though! Once we start petting Vinnie, he doesn't let us stop and will even try to climb onto our laps for some more love! Since Vinnie is **sixty pounds**, you can see how this might be a problem.

Vinnie fact #2

Vinnie loves to play!

What does he love to play with?

* my shoes,
* dolls,
* even unfriendly animals

In the battle between Vinnie and the skunk, who do you think won—

Vinnie or the **SKUNK?**

But most of all, he likes to play with us, his **people** family

and **them,**

his **four-legged gang**—who together wreak havoc all summer long. I'll introduce you to them in a moment.

With us, Vinnie likes to play fetch. If Vinnie is in the mood for fetch, he sneaks up, grabs something from us, and takes off. This will either get us to play fetch with him or get us to play his second favourite game,

tug-o'-war.

Either way, Vinnie wins.
I'd say he has us pretty well trained.

If we don't fall for his tricks and just put him outside he doesn't mind—

he'll play fetch by himself!

You can see him in the backyard, tossing things over his head and chasing them. It's quite a sight!

Now meet Vinnie's friends, the four-legged gang. They are all different shapes, sizes, and colours, and they have different personalities, but they don't care—they all have fun together no matter how different they are.

ATTENTION! I interrupt this story for the following tweet:

TOBY
-TERRIER-

Also known as Rat Dog. Why? He looks and smells like a rat. Why? He likes to roll in anything smelly. Toby is small, but don't let his size fool you. He is the leader of the gang and can be vicious. He is often seen barking orders. He's also very sneaky and can make a fast getaway.

TURTLE
-LAB-

Also known as The Distractor. She looks sweet and innocent, but don't let that fool you. Turtle will try to distract you from whatever you are doing by luring you to play fetch with the ball she constantly carries. Don't fall for it. It's a trick! She never lets go of the ball.

PARKER
-AKITA-

Also known as Parker Man. Why? I don't really know. Maybe it's because he's older than the others. Parker can usually be found lurking in the shadows and on the lookout. What's he on the lookout for? Spaghetti! Never leave your spaghetti unattended!

LILY
-HUSKY SHEPHERD-

Also known as Poopy Lily-Bea. Why? If you ate the things she does, you'd have to go to the bathroom a lot too. Lily eats anything from doors, to underwear, to makeup, to small animals. If you're missing something, chances are Lily ate it!

If you spot the four-legged gang, I strongly suggest you get out of the way . . .

or risk being **TRAMPLED!**

After a long play Vinnie is ready to sleep. But before he settles into a nap, he always comes to us for love. After all, love is what makes everyone feel good and Vinnie is no exception. So, with a few scratches here and a few pats there, Vinnie is happy and ready for bed.

He lies on his back and sticks all four legs straight in the air before falling fast asleep.

Sweet dreams, Vinnie!

There you have it! That's our dog, Vinnie, the best pest in the world! **(Oops, I meant pet.)** You may not think he sounds like such a troublemaker after all, but you've really only just met him. Wait till you find out what happened when he stayed home alone for the very first time.

But that's another story!

Dear Readers,

Before you go, I just wanted to say that Vinnie dropped a slobbery ball in my lap. Can you guess what he wants to do right now? Okay, Vinnie, let's go. Until next time.

♡ 6.5

CPSIA information can be obtained
at www.ICGtesting.com
Printed in the USA
LVIC06n0727081113
360273LV00003B/7